For James, Ben,
and Ella

First Edition

ISBN 0–316–73449–7

Library of Congress Catalog Card Number 90–53351

10 9 8 7 6 5 4 3 2 1

Published simultaneously in Canada
by Little, Brown & Company (Canada) Limited

Printed by Mandarin Offset
Printed and bound in Hong Kong

Two in a Pocket

Robin Ravilious

Little, Brown and Company
Boston Toronto London

One autumn, Snippet the dormouse curled up to sleep in a stack of straw in a field.

When she awoke in the spring, she found herself in a barn!

How could that be?

Had she been moved while she was asleep?
She felt bewildered and very hungry.
But there was nothing to eat except some stale seeds.

Suddenly she saw a face staring at her greedily through the window.

In a panic, she dived into the pocket of an old coat hanging on the wall.

To her surprise, she found herself in a nice warm nest,
so she made herself at home. But the nest belonged to
Jenny Wren, who was hopping mad!

"Thief! Burglar! *Pickpocket!* Get out this minute or I'll peck you to shreds!" she cried.

Snippet crept out and explained what had happened.
"Tut-tut," said Jenny, simmering down a little. "You'd
better stay here after all, because a cat lives in this garden
and he will get you."

"We'll share," Jenny decided. "You can sleep during the day while I'm out hunting spiders –"

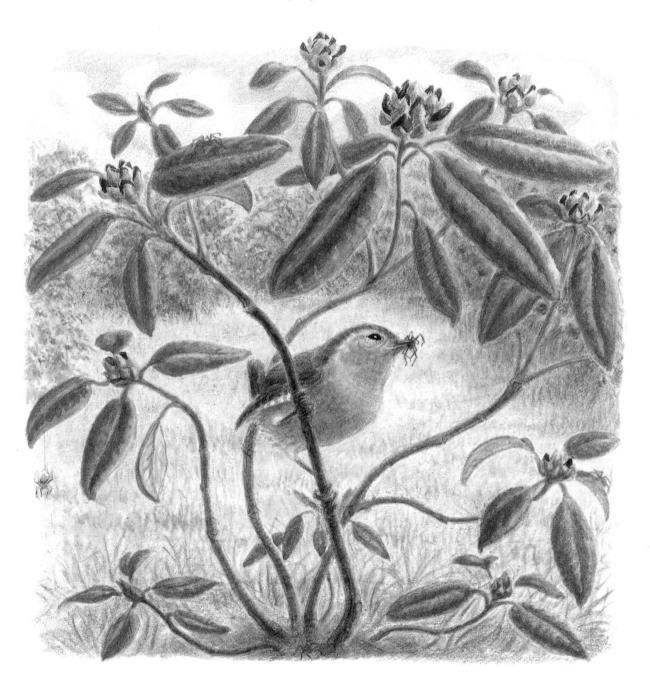

"And *you* can sleep at night while I look for shoots and blossoms in the moonlight!" said Snippet.

But sharing a house isn't so easy. If Snippet overslept,
Jenny was flustered. If Snippet ate nuts in bed,
Jenny became furious.

And Jenny sang so loudly in the mornings that Snippet
found it hard to get to sleep.

And then there was the cat.

He stalked Jenny by day.

And skulked after Snippet by night.

"Not a moment's peace," Jenny would say crossly.
Snippet longed for her old home in the fields.

Then one evening, Jenny didn't return to the nest.
A worried Snippet waited and waited, but still she didn't
come. What could have happened?

Then, over by the wall, Snippet saw the cat staring fiercely
at something caught in some netting.
Could it be Jenny?

It was!

Poor Jenny was in terrible trouble!

"Help me!" she gasped. "The cat pounced, and I flew straight into this net. I'll never get out alive!"

"Now, now," soothed Snippet. "What are my teeth for?
Leave it to me."
And she nibbled, and gnawed, and teased out the tangles
with her paws.

Snippet's heart thumped as she dragged Jenny to a hole in the wall.

She kept Jenny warm and bandaged her leg.
The cat couldn't reach them and went away in disgust.
They were safe.

At dawn, Snippet brought her patient plump grubs to eat
and dew to drink.

She even caught her a spider.
"What would I do without you?" sighed Jenny.

When Jenny was well again, she flew back to the nest.
"Now it's *your* turn to rest," she said when Snippet arrived.
"You must be worn out!"

Snippet had just dozed off when the nest began to lurch.
A man had taken down the coat and was carrying it away
– with Snippet fast asleep inside!
Jenny flew along behind, twittering with alarm.

The man reached a field and stopped. He took the coat and
draped it over a scarecrow.
"Wake up, sleepyhead!" shrilled Jenny when the man had
gone.
And Snippet found her dream had come true.
"It's my old field!" she cried.

Summer passed happily, for now there were lots of
wonderful things to eat. And no cats!

Snippet started to build herself a nest to be proud of – in
the *other* pocket of the coat.

Then, when winter came, Snippet said good night and
snuggled into bed.
"Sleep well, friend," said Jenny. "I'll keep you safe until
spring."
And Snippet drifted off to sleep to the sound of her friend
singing in the frosty air.